STECK-VAUGHN ✦ **BOLDPRINT** ✦

Glen Downey
Art by Hilary Jenkins

GRAPHIC READERS

Literacy Consultants
David Booth • Larry Swartz

Steck-Vaughn is a trademark of HMH Supplemental Publishers Inc. registered in the United States of America and/or other jurisdictions. All inquiries should be mailed to HMH Supplemental Publishers Inc., P.O. Box 27010, Austin, TX 78755.

Common Core State Standards © Copyright 2010. National Governors Association Center for Best Practices and Council of Chief State School Officers. All rights reserved. This product is not sponsored or endorsed by the Common Core State Standards Initiative of the National Governors Association Center for Best Practices and the Council of Chief State School Officers.

Ru'bicon www.rubiconpublishing.com

Editorial Director: Amy Land
Project Editor: Dawna McKinnon
Editor: Jessica Rose
Creative Director: Jennifer Drew
Art Director: Rebecca Buchanan

Printed in Singapore

ISBN: 978-1-77058-584-3
2 3 4 5 6 7 8 9 10 11   2016   22 21 20 19 18 17 16 15 14 13
A B C D E F G

CONTENTS

The Turners are pioneers traveling to their new home in Oregon. Jackson and Bess Turner are accidentally separated from their parents.

Will they make it on their own?

CHARACTERS

Mr. Turner

Mrs. Turner

Jackson

Bess

In 1853, the Turner family was moving from Missouri to Oregon. Other members of their family had already settled there.

DID YOU KNOW?

During the 1800s, pioneers moved to Oregon because the land was free. The trip from the East could take five to eight months. People carried their belongings in a covered wagon and walked next to it.

Ma looked back to see if Pa was okay.

Jackson and Bess ran as fast as they could without looking back.

When they stopped to catch their breath, they realized Ma was no longer behind them!

Wait, Bess. Where's Ma?

Shhh! We can't let those men hear us. Don't worry, she'll catch up to us.

An hour later, the sky was getting darker, and there was still no sign of Ma and Pa.

MA!

PA!

I'm so thirsty.

Come on. I think I hear running water. Maybe there's a stream close by.

It's right over here. Careful — watch your step!

Jackson finally fell asleep, but Bess did her best to stay awake.

Early the next morning, Jackson and Bess were approached by a young girl.

Oh, no! I must have fallen asleep.

With a shock, Bess noticed the surprise visitor.

Who are you?

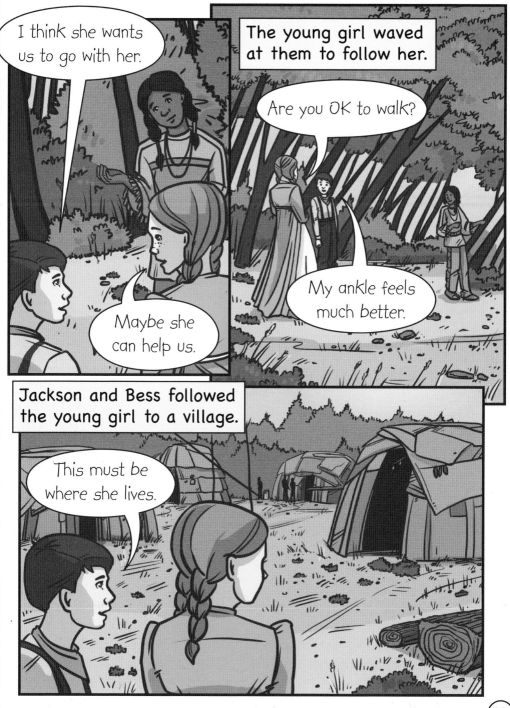

They were greeted by the young girl's father.

My name is Bess, and this is my brother Jackson. We're lost. We were going to our new home with Ma and Pa.

The girl's father led Jackson and Bess into the village for a meal.

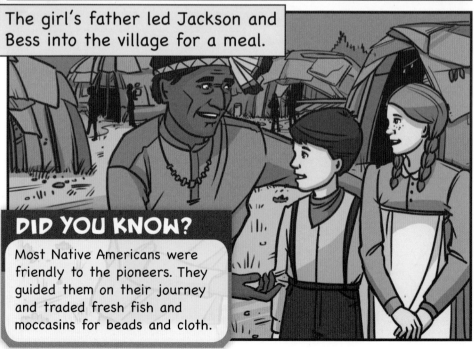

DID YOU KNOW?

Most Native Americans were friendly to the pioneers. They guided them on their journey and traded fresh fish and moccasins for beads and cloth.

After their meal, Bess and Jackson prepared to continue their journey. The father offered to show them the way back through the woods.

As they made their way through the woods, Bess and Jackson heard a scream in the distance.

HELP! HELP!

Quick! Follow me! That sounds like Ma!

Bess and Jackson were worried their parents might be in trouble.

Hurry, Jackson!

HELP! HELP!

Which way do we go?

This way! Hurry!

MA!

All of a sudden, the sound of horses scared away the bear.

Jackson and Bess were finally reunited with their parents.

The Turners bid farewell to their new friends.

Thank you so much for helping our children find us.

Then the family set out for Oregon.

Other members of the Turner family were waiting for them when they arrived.

Where have you *been*? We were expecting you yesterday!

It's a long story!

Bess and Jackson explored the settlement where their family planned to build their new home.

Then they settled down for a meal.

DID YOU KNOW?

When pioneers arrived in Oregon, they had to clear land and build a log cabin. If they were lucky, they had family already there and could live with them while building their house.

Comprehension Strategy:
Summarizing

beginning   middle   end

Common Core Reading Standards
Informational Text
4. Determine the meaning of general academic and domain-specific words and phrases in a text relevant to a grade 3 topic or subject area.
6. Distinguish their own point of view from that of the author of a text.
7. Use information gained from illustrations (e.g., maps, photographs) and the words in a text to demonstrate understanding of the text
8. Describe the logical connection between particular sentences and paragraphs in a text
9. Compare and contrast the most important points and key details presented in two texts on the same topic.
10. By the end of the year, read and comprehend informational texts

Reading Foundations
Word Study: Suffixes
High-Frequency Words: animal, catch, different, early, family, father, finally, follow, food, hope, hour, river, sound, stay, water, without
Reading Vocabulary: continue, galloping, journey, message, offered, settlers, traveling, tripped, village, wagon, waved, worry
Fluency: Conveying Emotion and Feeling

BEFORE Reading

Prereading Strategy   Activating Prior Knowledge
- Introduce the book by pointing to the picture on the cover.
- Invite students to discuss what they think the people in the wagon are doing. Then ask them to discuss the meaning of the word *settler*.

Introduce the Comprehension Strategy
- Point to the Summarizing visual on the inside front cover of this book. Say: *Today we will practice summarizing. When you summarize, you retell only the most important ideas of a story. Every story has a beginning, middle, and end.*
- On the board, draw a rectangle, divide it into three parts, and label them "Beginning," "Middle," and "End."
  Modeling Example Say: *I will use the organizer to summarize. As I read, I will think about important events from each part of the story. To help figure out a story's beginning, middle, and end, I look to see if it is divided into chapters. When I finish reading, I will write important events from this chapter in the first part of the organizer.* Point to the Beginning section.
- Say: *Good readers summarize after reading because summarizing helps us understand what we read. Summaries are short.*